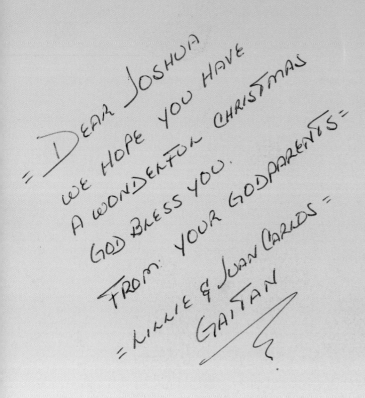

= Dear Joshua
We hope you have
a wonderful Christmas
God bless you.
From: your godparents =
= Lillie & Juan Carlos =
Gaitan

To Rob Lunde for letting us use his cool idea—S.B. and J.K.
To my wife, Lois, who is always there for me. Thanks—Garry

Text copyright © 2001 by Sylvia Branzei and Jack Keely. Illustrations copyright © 2001 by Garry Colby. All rights reserved. Published by Price Stern Sloan, a division of Penguin Putnam Books for Young Readers, New York. Printed in Hong Kong. Published simultaneously in Canada. No part of this publication may be reproduced, stored in any retrieval system, or transmitted, in any form or by any means, electronic, mechanical, photocopying, recording or otherwise, without the prior written permission of the publisher.

Library of Congress Cataloging-in-Publication data is available.

ISBN 0-8431-7682-2   A B C D E F G H I J

THE DINOSAUR STORE

Written by **Sylvia Branzei** and **Jack Keely**
Illustrated by **Garry Colby**

PSS!
PRICE STERN SLOAN

"Guess what?" said Skip. "I'm getting a pet."

Violet guessed. "A kitty? A pony? A pig?"

"Nope," said Skip, "a DINOSAUR!"

So, Skip and Violet went to The Dinosaur Store. The Dinosaur Store was one of the biggest buildings in Eurekaville. It had to be huge to hold all of the dinosaurs.

DIPLODOCUS
(di PLOH de cuss)
Longest dinosaur—90 ft. from head to tail.
Suitable for owners of basketball courts.

There were many
kinds of dinosaurs.

BOOKS

SALE

You
Are Here
✗

on sale
COMPSOGNATHUS
(komp sow NAY thus)
Chicken-sized meat-eaters
Caution—we bite!

Map

Some were big.
Some were small.
Some were long,
and some were tall.

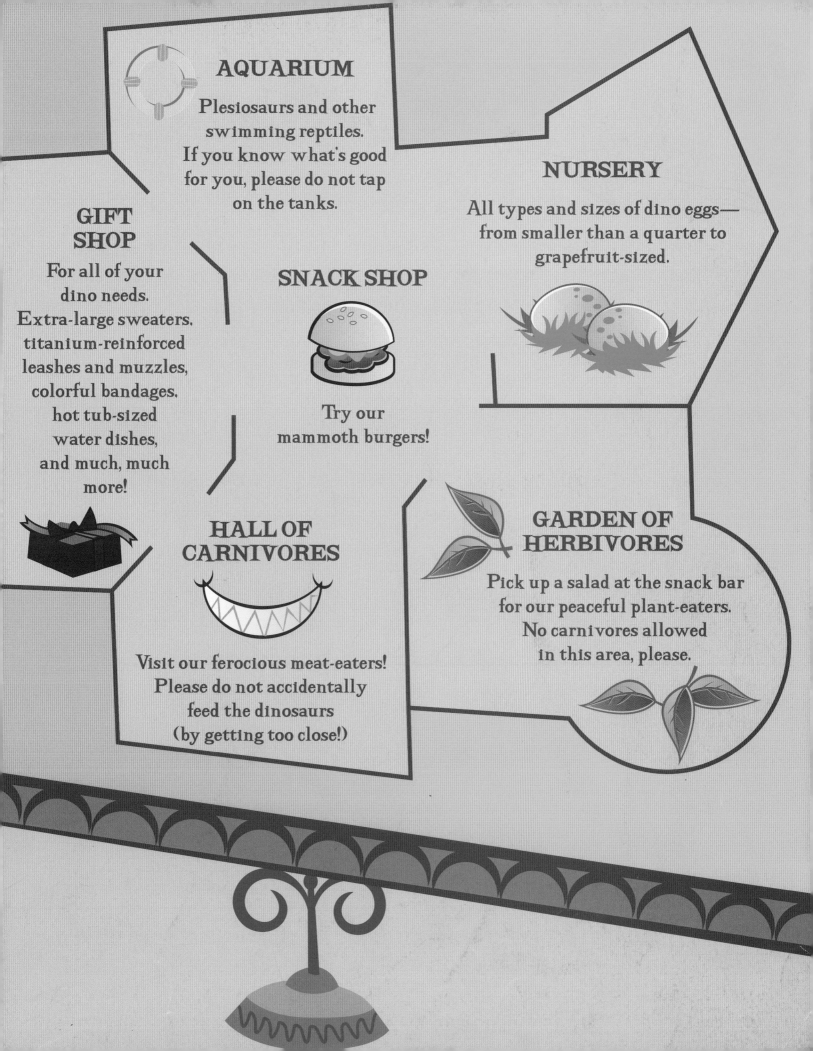

AQUARIUM

Plesiosaurs and other
swimming reptiles.
If you know what's good
for you, please do not tap
on the tanks.

NURSERY

All types and sizes of dino eggs—
from smaller than a quarter to
grapefruit-sized.

GIFT
SHOP

For all of your
dino needs.
Extra-large sweaters,
titanium-reinforced
leashes and muzzles,
colorful bandages,
hot tub-sized
water dishes,
and much, much
more!

SNACK SHOP

Try our
mammoth burgers!

HALL OF
CARNIVORES

Visit our ferocious meat-eaters!
Please do not accidentally
feed the dinosaurs
(by getting too close!)

GARDEN OF
HERBIVORES

Pick up a salad at the snack bar
for our peaceful plant-eaters.
No carnivores allowed
in this area, please.

"What kind of dinosaur would you like to get?" asked Violet.

"I would like a huge dinosaur—Tyrannosaurus rex," said Skip "I could ride him like a cowboy."

"T. rex is a fierce hunter," said Violet.
"He might forget you are his friend..."

"...and think you are a snack!"

"I think I would like a plant-eating dinosaur better," said Skip. "Maybe a large plant-eater like Apatosaurus."

TODAY ONLY

SOLD

BIG DINO SALE

RAISE YOUR OWN

DO NOT FEED

"He is much too big for a house. Where would you keep him?" asked Violet.

"In my yard," said Skip.

APATOSAURUS
(a PAT oh sore us)

Formerly known as Brontosaurus.
Can reach lengths up to 90 ft.
Very large appetite.
Huge yard required.

"What would he eat?"
asked Violet.
"He could eat the shrubs
and the grass," said Skip.

"Apatosaurus eats over a half ton of plants a day,"
said Violet. "There wouldn't be a lawn left in Eurekaville!"
"Maybe I don't want a really big dinosaur after all,"
said Skip. "I know! How about a baby dinosaur?"

At the nursery, a mud nest of Maiasaurs had just hatched.

"These newborn dinosaurs would be like raising a baby chick right from the egg," said Skip.

"They are not exactly cute," said Violet.

MAIASAURS

(MY a sores)

The name means "mother lizard."
A nice gift for that special mom.

"I think I would like a baby Stegosaurus," said Skip.

"He's rather sweet," admitted Violet. "But a grown-up Stegosaurus would not be very fun to pet."

10%
OFF

T-REX

Big Pets

think big

Big Pets

T-REX

think big

StEGoSAuRuS

(STEG oh sore us)

Armor develops as
dinosaur matures.
Has a brain the size
of a meatball.
Difficult to train.

There were dinosaurs honking through horns on their heads. And dinosaurs swinging the clubs on their tails.

HoNK

honk

PARASAUROLOPHUS
(PAR a sore ol o fus)

Noisy dinosaur. Honks through a crest on the top of head. Not appropriate for schools, hospitals, or libraries.

ANKYLOSAURUS
(ang kyl oh SORE us)

Slow moving. Swings club tail when threatened. Needs gentle training. Be sure to wear our Anky Trainer's Pads.

There were nasty dinosaurs with sails on their backs. And plant-eating dinosaurs with spikes on their beaks.

SOLD

SPINOSAURUS
(spy no SORE us)

The 6 ft. sail on its back makes this intelligent 7 ton killer, a decorative, if challenging, addition to your family.

MARKED DOWN

STYRACOSAURUS
(sty rak oh SORE us)

Name means spiked lizard. Wear gloves!

In the aquarium, creatures
paddled about.
  "Look at these, Vi," said
Skip. "It might be fun
to have a water friend."

SALE!

BIG DINO CHOW

SALE

KEEP HANDS
OUT OF WATER

"They don't look so friendly to me," said Violet. "And you'd need a *huge* bathtub to hold one."

Skip frowned. "There has to be a creature here somewhere that will make a good pet."

PLESIOSAURS
(PLEE see oh sores)
AND
ICHTHYOSAURS
(ICK thee oh sores)
Marine reptiles.
Not actually dinosaurs but still big and dangerous.
Keep your hands out of the water.

PTEROSAURS

(TEAR oh sores)

Things with wings.
Must jump from high places.
Suitable for living on the top floor
of high-rise apartments.

In the rooftop aviary, pterosaurs flapped their wings.

"I know what I want," said Skip. "A flying cousin of the dinosaurs will make a perfect pet."

"But some pterosaurs have a wingspan the size of a small plane!" said Violet.

"Not one of *those* dino cousins, silly," said Skip. "One of these!"

BiRDS

Modern-day cousin
of the dinosaurs.

"Some dinosaurs may have had feathers," said Skip, "And over a long, long time, they changed into birds."

"We did it, Skip," laughed Violet. "We have the perfect pet dinosaur!"